Growing Up Naked

The Untold Stories of Children at War

By Mc-Anthony Keah

PublishAmerica
Baltimore

First printing

This is a work of fiction. Names, characters, places, and incidents either are the product of the author's imagination or are used fictitiously. Any resemblance to actual persons, living or dead, events, or locales is entirely coincidental.

ISBN: 1-60813-334-6
PUBLISHED BY PUBLISHAMERICA, LLLP
www.publishamerica.com
Baltimore

Printed in the United States of America

For Annette Nettie Note

CHAPTER ONE

Oldpa became a child soldier at the age of nine. Driven from their home in fear of their lives he and his mother and father had taken refuge at a local church a few kilometers from their home. But they were not alone. Thousands of other families also took refuge in the church. Its huge compound compensated for the lack of rooms to host the many other families that had gathered there. St. Peter's, as it was known to the locals, was the only church that had its gates open and many families and individuals had gathered there for various reasons. While some people enter the gates of the church in search of protection from the blood-thirsty army of the falling government, many others enter in search of food because a relief organization was providing free food to displaced people. The stores and marketplaces were looted of everything. Money became useless as the rich and the poor lay bare in desperation. As more and more people's homes were abandoned the church compound became overcrowded.

But St. Peter's Church safe haven had only lasted a few gracious weeks when soldiers of the disappearing army of the government stormed its gates. Like most of the continent, the civil conflict in this tiny African country had begun on a tribal note. The government took no chances and those perceived to be enemies were searched in their homes and killed. But as the compound of St. Peter's overflowed with families and individuals seeking protection and food, so too were the homes becoming empty. Thousands of vulnerable people sat under the clouds hoping that God would hear their prayers and save their lives. The answer to that prayer did not come soon enough for Oldpa and his family. In a brutal murder that lasted for many hours on the night it took place, he lost both his parents.

The night before the massacre, Oldpa had not been able to sleep. He lay in his bed as though in the open sky waiting for the morning not knowing what would happen during the night. That night as he prayed feeling heavy in his body, he felt like he had a burden to carry. Unfortunately, this was not one of the quiet and peaceful nights that he was born into. Those nights he would stay there in his bed singing Christian songs of praises in his heart and hoping for the bright and sunny morning when he would eat breakfast in haste, take his shower, grab his books and run to school to see those friends that he missed dearly. This night was one of the many other nights that troubled his mind since the civil war began. It was a night when the sound of machine guns shattered the air.

Oldpa struggled to pull himself from among the bodies that surrounded him that morning. He got up despite a bullet wound in his right hand. He knew immediately that now was the time when he had to fend for himself. He ran for his life and for survival. His flight did not last for long when he came across commandos of one of the many rebel factions fighting the government army.

He took up arms and became a soldier and a commando himself. But to Oldpa's amazement, he was not alone. Like him, many other children made the same journey. They were on the battlefield daily fighting for revenge and for survival. Many other children lost their parents the way it happened to him. In the scorching sun he stood in formation like all the others. The wind ruffled the edges of their bewildered shadows as men in army uniforms moved around giving instructions in loud tones. Then one of the men said, "You have all come to the right place comrade…you all made the right choice. Stand up and fight for your parents, brothers and sisters and for your country. Rise, comrades, rise, your struggles are over, our battles are already won…"

Oldpa stood stilled and perplexed. He realized suddenly that the training camp was certainly not a place for children or child's play. It was the rebel training ground. The commandos repeated slogans and chanted words as the rebel army grew larger and larger with more children enlisted.

In this rebel army like many others, it was only a matter of days to complete training and be sent to the battlefield. Oldpa was a fierce fighter and he had distinguished himself throughout the training and the attacks that follow on two separate battlegrounds. His peers called him "gena" to depict that he killed enemy soldiers before they knew it. He soon became a senior commander for the small boys' unit, a division of children fighting in the rebel army. The same unit was also known as the border patrol because it patrolled all the border crossings and had engaged in cross-border fighting. In the neighboring country, Sierra Leone where border patrol was engaged in a fight, he met Kaba who later became his good friend and a comrade in arms.

Like Oldpa, Kaba was an ordinary twelve-year-old boy who lost both his parents after the war began in Sierra Leone. He locked himself up for three months until all his food was exhausted. When he decided to take a walk down the street in search for food, he met a rebel army commander who told him to join her truck when he asked her for some food. He never made it back home. He became her personal bodyguard and fought most of the major wars within the country and later in neighboring Liberia and the Ivory Coast. When Kaba met Oldpa he soon found out that they both had similar stories of how they lost their parents and how they came to join the rebel armies.

The two boys would spend mornings and evenings talking about their experiences and the people they had killed. For this kind of discussion helped them identified with each other. Only the two of them knew to what extent they were losing their childhood. And they also knew why they were carrying the big guns that were so heavy and almost dragging to the ground, but had to be carried. And though people would look at them with pity and would imagine to know their stories better, only the two of them knew where and how far they had come. And only the two knew where they were headed. Sometimes just to make conversation, they would ask each other about how the other became a soldier or a "freedom fighter" as they were told.

In the beginning of their journey, the adult commanders would tell them that they were more important and superior to anybody who did not carry a gun. They were told that a civilian, whether old or young, was inferior to them and in no way would measure up to them. Then the commanders would take them to a village or a town or a house. He or she would tell them to kill the inhabitants so as to formally establish his superiority over all other humans. In Oldpa's case he was made to kill a town chief and his family and burn all of their belongings. His commanders stood outside waiting for him. Then when he had finally done it, when he had shot the chief in front of his family and later killed the rest of them, he proceeded to set the house ablaze. He recorded later that he could still hear some people screaming and crying for their lives when he set the house on fire, but they all stood there with their guns pointed to the house to shoot any survivor who attempted to escape. But no one ran out. The chief and his entire family were already dead and the fire made ashes of their bodies. Then his commander shook his hand and congratulated him. He said to him that he was a brave and fierce fighter and the enemy would never overcome him. He had made his mark. He had established his superiority and it was time to move on to higher grounds.

In his many explanations to Kaba, Oldpa always said he was "lucky" that he did not really know the people he killed, or else he would have never been able to sleep for even an hour. Even though he was troubled that he killed these innocent people, not during enemy attack or major offences, he was greatly traumatized by the event. Others weren't so lucky. They were forced to kill a best friend or a boy like themselves. These were the people that he pitied. He could not imagine how they slept or ate. For his part, sometimes he was able to say to himself, *I did not know them, I had not seen them before.*

But all these events were in the past now. The war had ended and Oldpa, a traumatized boy who became a child soldier at the age of nine, was seventeen years old and going through his second round of counseling. In other to be de-traumatized the usual post-traumatic stress disorder had to be administered. He had done it before and he was doing it again, this time mostly in the form of interview. And so it was, Oldpa stood before a counselor to be rehabilitated. He was being asked to tell his story like he remembered in the hopes that it would de-traumatize him. He tried to utter a few words and stop. He looked around the room to see if there were others listening to him. But it was just him and his counselor and no one else. And then be began telling his story in the order that it had occurred. The order that he thought he remembered vividly on that fateful night when the soldiers had brutally and indiscriminately killed those perceived to be the enemy of the government and those who were thought to be helping the rebels make advances on the city. They had killed women and children who had taken up refuge at St. Peter's Church compound and Oldpa's parent were among those who were killed.

"I saw my mother sitting on the floor. She had been shot. Her two legs were broken. I think my father got shot too but I did not see his body. Maybe he escaped. Almost all the men in the compound were killed except for the few that were able to escape before the soldiers saw them. I did not see my father or his body when I ran for my life. There were too many bodies all over the place. I ran outside but I could not do anything for my mother."

"Wait…wait, please do not speak too fast. I want you to take your time. We have all day and the day after and so forth. So you said you saw your mother sitting on the floor. She had been shot, and then what happened? Actually, do you remember what happened before your parents decided to move to the compound? Do you remember anything at all?" the counselor asked.

"I do not remember much but you know when the war began, the government soldiers were killing people. Anybody who they thought was not supporting the government was an enemy and they killed or tried to kill them. Many people were dragged away from their homes, from the streets and even from workplaces. They were taken to remote places and killed and buried in one big grave."

"When we saw the soldiers walking in our neighborhood my father did not like it. He said maybe they were preparing to come for us too. That's how my father suggested that we should move to the church compound. He said maybe God would protect us there. That's how we went to the compound. We stayed at the compound until…"

"Okay, hold on for a second, Oldpa," the counselor interrupted. "Let's start this again. So what happened when you first got to the compound? Tell me how you and your parents settled in the compound. How did you live and what happened before the night the soldiers came to kill people at the compound?"

The boy seemed like he could not utter any more words about the church massacre that left both his parents dead. His breath was short of speaking and his eyes told the rest of the story. As though overwhelmed by fear he put his hand in the back pocket of the jeans he wore and brought up a picture. He took few steps forward and handed the picture to the counselor. But instead of looking at the picture, she thought this was the right time to properly introduce herself and tell the boy her name, something she had failed to do earlier.

"My name is Cindy. I am from Canada and I am just a psychology student. Please do not be afraid of me. I am here to help you, Oldpa. I would like us to talk freely to one another." She paused and slowly glanced at the picture the boy handed her. It was a picture of a little kid, a child whose posture narrated a struggle with death. He had a bandage tied to his right hand. As Cindy lowered the picture from her face, she recognized that the little boy was Oldpa at a young age. She stared at him with empathy and was tempted to ask about the bandage stained with blood tied to his hand and what may have gone wrong. But his response was obvious. She knew he was shot. He had escaped death narrowly; the kind of death his mother and father had suffered in his presence. He survived.

9

Outside the building where the counseling session with Oldpa was taking place, another man, one of the locals, was telling his story to the lady who had accompanied Cindy. She too, like Cindy, looked curious and wanted to help. She was trying to make sense of the chaos and give what little help she could to the young people who had been affected in this war-torn country. But as she stood listening to the man, she soon began to realize that the problem was immense. Too many of the young boys and girls needed help. Though not all of them were child soldiers, all of them were affected by the war. Everyone in this part of the world must have a story, she thought, or more specifically, a unique story.

The wind blew softly and tenderly, leaving her dress flying from one end of her body to the other. The West Africa she had read about in all the books she bought and borrowed from the libraries seemed to look different in reality. The children, the young boys and girls, the wind, the stories and the people were all alive and not in the books this time. Reality had taken hold of her and she, like others before her, had begun to wonder if she had made the right choice to come here.

The lady lifted up her head and stood up straight as she continued to listen to the man.

"I too, like Oldpa, was a child soldier," he said. "Now I am twenty years old, but I began fighting when I was thirteen years old."

"Who is Oldpa?" the lady interrupted.

"Oldpa is the boy that your friend is talking to in this building—"

"So you know Oldpa?" she interrupted again.

She had learned that in these war-torn countries, some young people fabricated stories about their military involvement in order to attract attention. Some even went as far as lying about being child soldiers to attract international NGO help. Maybe this was a good opportunity to test Oldpa's story, she thought. Maybe he could be lying or fabricating his story to Cindy.

"Oldpa is my pekin," the man continued. "I saw the site of the massacre and the dead bodies and Oldpa's mother sitting on the floor in the pool of blood surrounded by bodies. I was not able to save her. But later, both of us were child soldiers and he was the commander for our unit."

"Wait! You said too many things at one time. I don't understand. What massacre and what do you mean by pekin?"

"Oh, I am sorry. I thought you knew about the massacre. That's where it all started...our journey into the rebel army. It was in St. Peter's Church compound where Oldpa and his parents took refuge because of fear from being attacked by the government army; I was there also with my mother. My father was killed earlier when he was on his way from work. He went to work and never made it back home. My mother decided that we should go to the church compound and seek refuge and so we did. That is where I met Oldpa.... The church compound is also where the government soldiers came and killed so many people that they thought were enemies of the government....

"Pekin means small boy in the local language but we used it sometimes even if the person was about the same age as you."

"So what else do you know about this pekin?" the lady asked in a monotone.

By this time she was beginning to take interest in the conversation. She knew that whatever this man told her could serve as a justification for Oldpa's story. Her dress was soaking wet from the West African heat. The manmade dry monsoon wind blowing from the east known here as the hamanttan brought little relief and sign of hope. It almost seemed like the sweating would go away and her somewhat missionary dress would give her body a little more freedom. Her lips were beginning to dry up and soon the dust from the ground started to make its way up in her face. She stood there by the side of the house where Cindy continued to question Oldpa.

"So if I told you everything I know about Oldpa, will you take me abroad too? I mean to the United States?"

"No! No, we are not here to take people abroad. We just want to help counsel young people who were affected by this war. Actually you may have to talk to my friend Cindy who is talking to Oldpa. But maybe not today because it is getting dark and she may be tired when the session when Oldpa is done.... Why don't we see you another time when we will all be energized and we could talk for a longer time? The day is almost over now."

The lady had barely completed her sentence when Cindy walked out of the building with Oldpa. Darkness was falling quickly. It had been a beautiful day, a bright sunny day like most of the other days in this African country. There were not too many seasons here—two at the most—the dry and rainy seasons. *The sun was always up, so it must be the dry season,* Cindy thought when she looked up. The bright, hot and tiring rays from the sun brought hope to the land and its inhabitants.

There is so much to hope for here. It is so bright and hopeful. There

11

is no winter, spring or fall and everything is so light, bright and hopeful. How could such a place be referred to as a dark continent? She lifted up her head, gazing towards the heavens and discovered that the sun had suddenly disappeared. One shooting star dazzled its way into the clouds, then another and another. The stars attracted her attention as she stood completely gazing towards the heavens. And then in sweet lowly tones she heard voices singing. *Heaven must be joyful tonight and the angels of God can't hold it back,* she thought. *Oh my God! These people are so blessed that one can actually hear the voices of angels reaching down from heaven. I can hear the voices, angels of God from heaven singing. This is unbelievable,* she thought to herself again. Then the voices sounded close and loud and beautiful.

Cindy stood gazing into the heavens. As the singing got louder and louder, she soon realized that the voices were not coming from heaven; they came from the house across the street. She turned towards the house and gazed in amazed silence. As though still trumpeting from the heavens, the words of the song became all too loud and clear:

> This city of ours lies in ruin
> Our country and children are no more
> And though the world may have forgotten us,
> Our portion in heaven is made of gold
> Come ye children of the Lord and see why we joy.

CHAPTER TWO

In almost all instances all the child soldiers in African civil wars lost their parents and other family members and were in search of food or survival. Though in some instances single mothers would send their sons to join a rebel army so as to help feed the family, the greater need to survive forced the children into what became a vicious cycle. Children were unable to search for their parents or families without being killed. In almost all instances, they fell prey to fighting factions. These fighting forces then persuaded the kids to carry out revenge killings for their families and friends.

The man who was talking to Cindy's friend became a child soldier because his mother had asked him to do so. He had to help bring food for his younger brothers and sisters. In a family of six, at thirteen years old he was the oldest and had to become the breadwinner.

When Cindy and her friend returned to the building where she previously met with Oldpa for their second meeting they saw that the man was there waiting with some papers in his hand instead of Oldpa. He handed the paper to the lady upon saying hello and shaking their hands.

"I decided to write my story," he said, smiling at the woman. "I want to save you or your friend time. You don't have to stay here for many hours interviewing me or trying to counsel me. I have had some counseling in the past. So there you have it. The words on those papers say everything I have gone through. All the things that happened to me since the war began to the present time are all written on that paper. The words on that paper represent my life. This is my story."

The lady looked at the papers and look at the man's face. But he did not say a word again. He just stood there looking at Cindy and the lady anticipating their reactions. His eyes were dim and shackled. And he was staring as though with fear. He glanced at his watch and took a deep breath. He took two to three steps forward towards the lady in a passing motion and then stopped. He took another look at his watch, this time for a very long time. Then in a jerky motion he nodded his head, not saying a word. Cindy tried to say something about his watch in hopes of breaking the silence, but his back was already turned towards her.

The watch he wore was very beautiful and could raise a whole range of issues. The price, the glittering gold stripes and the brand were all very unique. It was a Rado. It was certainly a valuable possession to have. *Did he buy this watch with his own money? Did it belong to a rich family of his? Or did he rob someone, maybe a rich man, during the war when he was still a child soldier?* Cindy thought to herself. *Whatever the case, now was not the time to consider where he got his watch,* she thought again. This man had handed his story to the lady, her friend, and he was waiting for his interview. Or so he thought.

The lady took another look at the papers the man handed her and without a second thought began reading. At the very top of the first page he wrote in bold words what appeared to be the title of his story: "Growing Up Naked."

Before I became a soldier I lived with my mother and father. But when the war erupted my father never made it home from work on a fateful day that I will always remember. My mother decided that we should take refuge in St. Peter's Church compound to save our lives. We went to the church in haste leaving everything, and I mean everything, in our house. My mother did not want us to even attempt bringing the change of clothes. She said the government soldiers would have killed us if we wasted time dragging around the house until dark. "Food will be there," she said, "and all we need for now is food to survive until this madness is over."

When we arrived at the church many thousands of people already made it their home. There were people everywhere, pregnant women, single mothers and families. But like my mother said, there was plenty of food because a relief organization was providing food for everyone weekly. Allocations for sleeping were made according to gender and age.

The women and children slept in the rooms that were used as classrooms prior to the war. The men and older boys slept in the chapel and in the open space within the church compound. The men took turns keeping watch in case something bad was going to happen. Men who watch during the night divided themselves into two groups. Some of them sat on the top of the high walls made with bricks. That way they were able to see danger from afar and tell the other men that walked around within the compound. But on the night of the massacre, not one of them saw it coming. It all happened abruptly.

Just before nightfall on the night of the massacre, there were government soldiers roaming the street in the front of St. Peter's. They told the men sitting on the brick walls to get down and stay within the fence. They told them that they were there to protect us. The men believe them and got down from the high walls. They spread the news to the rest of the people that some government soldiers came to protect us. Many people did not believe what the soldiers said. There was fear and panic but some men who spent most of their day listening to the radio said it could be true. The government, they concluded, had been warned by the international community. They added that the United States had warned the government to stop the indiscriminate killing of civilians and ensured that those who are displaced receive protection.

We did not receive protection from the soldiers; they lied. They were part of the same group that committed the massacre. We were asleep in one of the rooms when the massacre took place. There was total darkness and the voices of women and children crying were repeatedly silence with machine guns. My mother held all of her children very tightly to herself. We were in one of the rooms squeezed against the wall almost suffocating from the stench of human blood. In a low voice she said, "It will be better if we die together." But we survived.

The next morning I saw the site of the massacre and the dead bodies and Oldpa's mother sitting on the floor in the pool of blood surrounded by bodies. I was not able to save her. Though she stretched out her hand and cried for my help, I ran for my life. I had to run. The government soldiers who had committed the massacre were going around in vehicles in an attempt to finish up those who had been shot but were still dragging from the compound to the streets. They were also gunning down people if they suspected that these were runaways from the compound.

Unlike Oldpa's mother, my mother made it out of the compound alive. We survived and walked for half a day to Bushord Islands. My mother encouraged me to join the rebel army because all my brothers and sisters were hungry and we had no food. I had to provide food for my sisters and brothers and so I joined the rebel army. But it was a gruesome experienced and I still despised it. I would never do it again if I don't have to. I saw and did many terrible things.

Almost all the kids in the Special Body (SB) Guard Unit that I served witnessed the brutal killings of people; they saw their parents, brothers, sisters and other relatives brutally murdered by government troops. Many felt they had to fight for survival. Many said they made the decision to fight to bring honor to their families and to their friends who had been killed. But nobody brought honor to their family by killing another person. I know this now but not then. The commanders or older folks took advantage of us in those days. They told us to bring honor to our parents and friends by taking revenge. They forced us to fight. Sometimes, the situation was so insane that we found ourselves fighting for the same group that harmed our friends and relatives and neighbors.

With the man's back still turned towards the lady, she kept reading his story. Every time she completed one paper, she passed it on to Cindy to read.

There are many different ways in which children are drawn into the fighting. Some of them are used to run errands in the beginning. They carried food on the war front, carried ammunition for weeks and months, acted as bodyguards to the senior and junior commanders, acted as spies, carried out reconnaissance, acted as informants, manned checkpoints and commanders' homes including their wife and children and carried out ambushes.

I remembered the two little girls that I met at the rebel army base when I first got there. They began by cooking. Their parents were killed during the war. Then one of the rebel factions that found them loaded them into a pickup truck like sardines along with some other children. They were told that they were going to send them out to another safe country to find families for them. In the back of the pickup truck, nobody saw them because it was covered up. It was not too long that they soon realized that the new country meant the army base and that new families also meant comrades-in-arms. There were people, young and old, men and women, running from one corner of the base to the other. Then as the girls recorded and narrated to me, they heard someone said to the driver of the pickup truck that drove them into the base, "We are under attack, move the cargo."

Then there was gunfire everywhere. They were told to lie down face-flat to the ground, right there, and not run or move until the firing stop. Two hours later, the enemy forces had been repelled.

"This is a base," another voice told them. "You will be safer here than any place."

At twelve years old they were put into the kitchen to cook for the boys after a long day at the front. There was always food in the kitchen to be cooked, so they never went hungry. But one day they noticed that the number of them in the kitchen had been reduced. There were fifteen girls in the beginning, but later there were seven. Nobody said anything but as the weeks went by, they saw a boy shot right in front of them. They were told he was an enemy soldier trying to infiltrate the base. The boy seemed to be about nine or ten years old. One single bullet right into his chest in the square and he was dead. His body lay there and then a few minutes later, the base commander brought them each an AK47 rifle and told them they might need it to protect themselves in the kitchen when cooking.

There was no further warning before they were told one morning at around 5:30 a.m. that there was a manpower shortage and that they would be needed at the front to help back up the soldiers. It later became a routine. Then one of the commanders decided to have sex with both of them after a long day at the front. He made one person watch while he forced his penis into the friend's vagina, twisting and turning her at his wish. She was screaming but he seemed to be enjoying himself and then he turned to the other friend and said to get ready. But she stood there looking disgusted at him. She got naked and walked towards them and she reached for the knife on the table and slashed his throat. Then she pulled her friend from under him and they began to run. They ran as far as the bridge over the St. Paul River that divided the base from the rest of the city and they slowed down.

The man's story went on and on, vividly describing horror upon horror and some of the realities of war that are almost never told. The ones that are almost always forgotten or when they are told, the public would assume that they do not make good reading. Some of the stories were from his personal experience, but some were also from the experiences of those that he met throughout his journey in the rebel army.

Meanwhile, as the lady and Cindy continued to read the man's story, Cindy was preparing and hoping that Oldpa would show up for their meeting to continue the counseling session. But at the house where Oldpa and Cindy were supposed to meet, he had not shown up. After two hours of waiting, the ladies decided to call it a day.

CHAPTER THREE

The voices sounded melodious and vibrant but the song was quite unique. Cindy thought she heard the same song sang once in her grandmother's church in Canada. And now, with the same tone it was being sung in West Africa by a group of people that the rest of the world would rather assume God might have forgotten. She stood as though frozen at the door of the church. Her body felt chilled and tiny little pimples covered her skin. Her feet became heavy and every part of her body seemed as though it had been left outside to freeze in the Canadian winter. The man at the entrance said to her to enter the church, to come in and the usher would lead her to her seat, but she stood still, gazing in amazement and humming the song along with the rest of the congregation while the lead singer sang: "Come, Ho-ly Spir-it, from Heav-en shine forth with your glo-rious light. Ve-ni Sancte Spir-itus. Come from the four winds, O Spir-it, come breath of God; dis-perse the shad-ows o-ver us, re-new and strength-en your peo-ple. Ve-ni Sanc-te Spir-I tus. You are our on-ly com-fort-er, peace of the soul. In the heat you shade us; in our la-bor you re-fresh us, and in trou-ble you are our strength. Ve-ni Sanc-te Spir-itus. Kin-dle in our hearts the flame of your love that in the dark-ness of the world it may glow and reach to all forever."

Written by a French composer Jacques Berthier who was born in 1923 at Auxerre Burgundy, "Veni Sancte Spiritus" is one of the many songs he wrote for the Taize community. A small but vibrant community of people, their song help changed a whole lot in many other communities in other parts of the world. The city and country where Cindy stood was no exception. Though its recent past may not have been a good representation of how much change any Christian songs may have achieved, its people knew God deep inside their

19

hearts and were always willing to voice it through songs.

"Oldpa, Oldpa," Cindy shouted. She ran towards the young boy sitting on the seat that was second to the last row and embraced him, trying to calm herself from the excitement. *Disturbance in the church is no fun especially when it comes from a stranger,* she thought. She looked around her and noticed that no one had actually taken notice of the loud way she shouted Oldpa's name.

"You are Oldpa, right?"

"Yes, I am Oldpa," the boy responded.

"I have been trying to find you everywhere since we last met. I want us to complete the counseling session we began. Can we meet after church?"

"OK."

Cindy had not seen Oldpa for the week and she had no way of getting in contact with him. Her contact that led her to the former child soldier could not find him either and her effort seemed to be coming to a dead-end when suddenly she ran into him at church.

"Good thing I came to church. Do you mind if I sit next to you?"

"No, sit down." His answers were very short.

"So would you like us to meet tomorrow, Oldpa?"

"Why do you want us to meet again? I thought I told you everything I had to say when we met?"

"You told me a lot and I appreciate that, but there are a few more questions I have to ask you, just a few more. Our time here is not long. I should be leaving to go back to my country sometime soon."

"So you are leaving? Leaving without me? I thought they told us that you came here to take some of us abroad. So you are taking other people with you and you don't want to take me?"

"No, Oldpa, who is they? Why would anyone say that to you? I am not taking anyone with me. I am—"

"But you want to take all our stories back to your country and write a book," the boy interrupted. "You come here and you take our stories and you don't do anything for us. That's all you people do. That's why my uncle said to not talk to you. I cannot talk to you anymore. I cannot tell you anything again. I don't want you to write my story in a book and make money while I suffer."

"Suffer?" Cindy asked.

"Yes, suffer, why you ask? You don't know what suffer means? It means hardship…hardship. I don't want to go through hardship while you enjoy yourself in your country with my story."

Perplexed, Cindy sat still looking the boy in the eye as he spoke his mind. She had noticed one thing in the few days and few weeks that she had been in the country. People here mixed the local English with Standard English. It sounded somewhat like the Black or African-American English but only a faster version.

"Enjoy myself with your story? Oldpa, what are you talking about? I am only a psychology student who came here to complete work for my thesis. I am also volunteering to make this a counseling session for you as well because I have some practical experienced in counseling. I am not one of those people who write books. I just want to help that's all."

"That's exactly what all of you say. I remembered the last woman said she was a student too. My uncle said not to talk to any of you again. He said I have told you enough."

"How about we talk about this after church, Oldpa?" Cindy asserted. "I think we are talking too loud in church and everyone is looking at us. Can we meet outside the church for a few minutes and talk after the service?"

"OK," the boy responded.

The melodious voices of the junior choir graced the end of Oldpa and Cindy's conversation as the pastor mounted the pulpit to deliver his Sunday message. The congregation hummed the song in preparation for prayer and then suddenly it was all quiet as the preacher talked about the need to repent and come back to God as a people and not allow the devil to use hatred for one another or to sow the seed of bigotry and destroy their country again.

The sermon came to an end and as the church sang the closing song, Cindy slowly made her way to the meeting spot where she had agreed to meet with Oldpa after the service. When Oldpa reached the meeting spot he appeared to be in a hurry to leave. However, Cindy in her calm gesture and charming smile managed to slow him down. The both agreed to a 1:00 p.m. meeting the following Monday and Oldpa left the building in haste.

Cindy thought about taking an afternoon nap as she stopped a local taxi heading back to her hotel. When she arrived at the hotel she ran through the lobby for fear that she might get caught up in a chat with the receptionist about how interesting the church service had been. But to her amazement someone shouted from the lobby as though to get her attention.

"Excuse me, ma'am," the voice said. She turned around to looked, and it was the man. He stood looking her straight into the eye and said, "Are you Cindy?"

"Yes, of course I am and I remembered you. So, how have you been?"

"I have been well," the man responded. And then in a polite voice as though seeking favoritism he said, "Did you read my story?"

"Oh yes! Your story, actually I have to admit I have not completed reading it, but I will ask my friend if she read all of it. I have to admit though that the little I read made so much impact on me. By the way," Cindy continued, "your English is more clear than most people here. How is that? Have you lived here all your life?"

"Yes, I have lived here all my life! But you have not met everyone in this country, have you?" the man asked. "I don't even believe you have met half of the population. How can you assumed that my English is clearer than many people? What is that supposed to mean?"

"Oh, please understand, I do not mean that. I was only complimenting you."

"Yes, but your compliment sounds like an insult to the rest of the people. You know," he continued, "I have problems with Westerners who come here or anywhere in Africa and think that the people are dumb or that no one speaks good English or everyone is dying and so forth. I hope you understand that this country, this place where you stand was established by Blacks, proud and free slaves from the United States of America. I hope you also understand that it means English has always been here from the get-go. English is also a mother tongue here.

"All you need to do is listen carefully to the people here when they speak and you will understand them. They may speak with an accent that you are not familiar with but you have to understand that you are in their country, you are the visitor, damn it, just listen to them and hear what they have to say. Stop judging whose English is clear and whose is not and so forth—"

"I think you are actually taking my comment out of context," Cindy interrupted as she watched the man in what seemed to be a fidgeting mood.

"I am not judging anybody nor am I concluding that the people here don't know how to speak English. I am happy to be here. I love the people here and I appreciate everything they have done for me since I got here. I also appreciate you for sharing your story with me. My friend appreciates you as well. I am sorry you misunderstood what I meant. I am really sorry."

"And what about my story, I guess you are also sorry you and your friend have not completed reading it. You keep it and write your book out of it. Come here and take our words and make fame for yourself while we remain hidden behind the curtains in the dark.

"While hard times continue to kill us, write our story and tell it in your own words. Do like the politicians do. Talk about some human-related, sophisticated political strategy and find a desk for yourself at the end of the day. Twenty years from now send your children, maybe your daughter, to come and listen to the same story, only this time not from me but maybe my son. And let her write her own book too and find a desk and continue the family fame."

As the man said these last few words to Cindy, he made for the exit sign swinging left and right at the hotel main entrance. She stood gazing as he disappeared into the thin air not even looking behind once.

In this part of the world people do not take speech lightly, she thought. *Or maybe it is just him.* Cindy recalled how she had made similar comments to many other people and not one of them reacted in the way he did or felt that she had insulted the rest of the population. She turned and walked towards her room.

She opened the door softly knowing that her friend could be dozing off to sleep. But the soft, tender opening did not serve its intended purpose. The lady jumped out of the bed as though awakened from a bad dream, and then looked at Cindy and said, "Oh, it's you."

"Yes, it is me. Is there something wrong?"

"No, no nothing. I am fine but I think we have to hurry up and leave this country, Cindy. It'd be good if we leave this week."

"What do you mean? We just can't leave like that. I still have interviews and other stuff to complete. And you, don't you have to transcribe all those tapes you have? Is there something you are not telling me?"

"I say we have to leave here this week. Do you hear me?" the lady shouted.

Still standing at the door and perplexed, Cindy thought to calm herself down to find out what has gotten into her friend. But before long, the lady shouted again, this time emotionally walking away from the bed toward Cindy and making a frantic gesture with the pillow in her hands.

"I said we have to leave this week…no later…do you hear me? I will be leaving this week and if you choose to stay then stay on, but I am leaving."

"Well, I am sorry, friend, but I am not…leaving," Cindy shouted back. "I have work to do here and until I complete my work, I am not going anywhere. You can leave all you want but I am not coming with you. I have too many people that I still have to meet. Most importantly I still want to meet Oldpa, you know, the young boy, the former child soldier? I am still counseling him. I can't just get up and leave.

"If you want to go back to Canada you may but just remember that you will be one of the reasons why people here think we only come here to make a living out of their stories and not actually listen to what they have to say.

"You know I saw—"

"I saw the man today," the lady interrupted before Cindy could say who she saw. "He did not look good. He looked angry and he scared me to death, Cindy. I don't know what to think but I seriously think that you should reconsider. I think we should leave here before something happens to one or both of us."

"I saw the man today too," Cindy replied to her friend's suggestion.

"Oh..., oh my! You saw him?"

"Yes, just when I about walked into the hotel entrance and was making my way to the room. I heard this person yell and when I turned it was him."

"How was he? Did he look calm or...?"

"No, well yes, he did look calm at first but then he took everything I said out of context and that's when he began accusing me of looking down on his countrymen and so forth. He got really angry and walked away mumbling words I could not understand."

"Did you complete reading his story?"

"Oh yes, his story, where is it? Let me see if I find it."

The lady grabbed the man's story from her back pack and they both continue reading where they left off.

They, the senior commanders in the rebel army, made us do everything and anything when we joined. And anyone who refused would be lucky to stay alive. I remembered they made us kill a boy... he may have been about eleven years old. We kicked him, beat him with sticks and spat on him because he refused to take the AK47 and kill the family that was the neighbor of his parents. Today I still dream of that boy and I can't justify to myself why we killed him. I see him in my dreams just standing there and staring at me.

We ran errands, we carried big guns and we were always in the forefront of every attack. If there were mines planted anywhere, they killed us first and if the enemy shot, we were the first to receive the bullets. We also guarded the senior commander's family.

Our experiences during and after the war are more than struggles, more than just trauma. We are left with many physical pains and we are handicapped both in our hearts and on our bodies.

Our stories are many and varied. The issue of child soldiers is just one of them. So when you write your book, remember to include some of the other stories, the untold ones you saw and experienced during your time in this country. Write some good things about us, not just our dark side. For everyone and everything have two sides to it, even your own people and country.

CHAPTER FOUR

Cindy and her friend sat on their beds in their hotel room pondering on the man's story. Her friend kept reading the story over and over trying to figure out in her head what in the story could be connected to his recent attitude and the anger he had channeled in the words he spoke to them separately. She kept thinking maybe there was a clue written on one of these papers. *He probably expected us to pick up on it,* she thought.

She knew that this man was once a child soldier. She also knew that he had undergone the post-traumatic stress disorder or PTSD program right after he was disarmed. He had mentioned this to her in one of their earlier conversations. What she did not know was how the program had helped him overcome the trauma he went through as a child soldier. She also did not know what stage he was at in his healing process. The more she read the man's story, the more she was attracted to his elegant style of writing. She was unable to pick up any hints about his recent actions. His story was so beautifully written it said very little of his experiences in the war personally. He wrote his experiences within the context of other children, both boys and girls, who had been taken advantage of and pressed into becoming child soldiers.

Was he trying to say something about his society in general? Or did his repeated reference to "we" or the "other children" in his story and then later "our people" in verbal conversations to Cindy and myself meant something else? Is he just frustrated with the situation around him or is he still deeply traumatized? Despite all these questions going through her head, the lady was unable to come up with any answers in her mind over the man's behavior. With her face buried in both hands, she sat on the bed in her own frustration as though waiting for a miracle to happen and bring her some answers.

26

Cindy for her part had chosen not to think too much about the man's behavior. She had decided not to attach too much meaning. Instead she thought his story and his behavior could be defined in the context of a larger picture of what other African children go through from time to time and how it grows with them into their young adult and adult lives. She read much literature on civil wars and conflicts in Africa and for her the only difference now was that what she read in the books was alive in her face. In her readings few authors had prepared her for what now was before her, the one writer had vividly described for her what to expect. "African societies in their state of poverty and warfare continue to mistreat their children," the writer wrote. "Increasingly the number of children used as combatants in almost every African civil war and struggle continues to rise. Children in Africa are being traumatized because of civil wars and poverty raging through the region. From Mozambique to the Democratic Republic of Congo, through the tender land of Uganda, Liberia, Sierra Leone and the Ivory Coast, children continue to suffer mental, emotional and physical pain from war and poverty," the writer concluded.

Cindy wrote down many quotations from many of the books she read, something that she knew would prove useful when it came time to write her paper. But now the words from those writers were making more sense now that the situation was bare right in her face.

In another article from the *New York Times* the journalist had attempted to draw the attention of the international community in the hope that they would help bring some relief for the children of West Africa. In the article the journalist had written, "One's eye roams the international community in quest for a government, an agency, a stronger international force. Or maybe someone, something, that could at least bring safety for the threatened children of these countries."

"Africa," another writer stated, "is poor and its population is young. Despite this poverty and most of the population of the continent being at a young age, civil war continues to rage. The leaders of the land have not been able to transform the vast energy coming from the vibrant youth into something positive. Instead, they, the youth, are left to swagger through the streets of their cities and towns and villages, looking for a reason and a place to belong. Take a walk along the streets of West African villages and cities, you will see thousands and thousands of young people and children sitting and waiting for their calling. Because the constructive society has not called them, the

27

destructive will call them. They will give them a meaning to life and tell them you had better do this than do nothing. They, the youth, in return will accept this calling because they have absolutely nothing to look forward to if they refuse this calling.

"Children in Africa continue to be the victims of problems on the continent. When greedy men want power to satisfy their greed and make wars, the children become the victims. When evil rapes a country apart in the form of apartheid, the children become the victims. When poverty ruins the streets of African villages, townships and cities, the children become the victims. As though this pain is not unbearable enough, children are the unseen, silent and the unspoken voices in the time of peace. They are always represented in the books, at the conferences and meetings and everywhere."

Written in black pen covering over ten to fifteen pages of the special notebook that she bought to use as a journal for her trip were one, two or three paragraphs taken from articles she had read. She sat there patiently listening to herself. Listening to what she always thought were the inner voices that bring calm in times of disturbances. As she read through the quotes over and over, reading her favorite ones two to three times in her head, she suddenly remembered the appointment with Oldpa when they met at the church. He had not guaranteed her that he was going to show up but she had to take her chances because she needed to talk to him. She stood up abruptly and said to the lady, "I have to meet with Oldpa. Do you wanna come? It's okay if you are not up to it, I will understand."

"I will come with you," the lady said. "Let me put some water on my face. I will be with you shortly," she said to Cindy in a fainting voice as she made for the washroom.

CHAPTER FIVE

Twenty minutes after Cindy and the lady had been waiting at the building where she and Oldpa had agreed to meet, a young woman between the age of eighteen and twenty showed up. She wore a "lappa," a unique piece of cloth around her waist covering most of her legs and her hair were braided in cornrows.

"Are you Cindy?" the young lady gestured.

"Yes, I am," Cindy answered. "I am not sure we have met before, have we?"

"Oldpa said he wants you to come to our house. He can't meet with you here today," the young lady in the lappa asserted to Cindy.

"Is everything okay with Oldpa? Or is there something wrong?"

"No, nothing is wrong with Oldpa; he wants you to come, that's all."

"Okay, I guess you will lead the way? Is the house far away from here?"

"No! It is just behind the big trees over there."

When Cindy and the lady got to Oldpa's house the area was crowded with so many people. Men, women and children stood outside chatting with one another in low voices.

"Oldpa, Oldpa," the young lady who led Cindy and her friend yelled. "There is Oldpa. I think he didn't hear me. Let me go and tell him you are here."

The young lady made her way swiftly within the crowd and tapped Oldpa's shoulder. When he turned around she said to him, "Your friends are here. I brought them."

Oldpa ran to greet Cindy and the lady. His mood was somber and he looked as though he had been crying.

"Is everything okay, Oldpa?" Cindy asked the former child soldier. "You look like you have a lot of people visiting your house?"

"My uncle died yesterday," the boy responded in a broken voice.

"Oh my God! I am so sorry to hear that. I was hoping to see your uncle one of these days before leaving. What was his name?"

"His name was Peterguy. He was very smart. All our family depended on him for direction."

"Peterguy?" Cindy's friend interrupted. "It sounds very much like the name the man told me on the first day I met him."

"The man? Who is the man?" Oldpa asked.

"Cindy and I met this man who said he knew you. He said he was also a child soldier and he was part of the same unit that you commanded during the war. He also said he was at the St. Peter's compound but only with his mother."

"And both of us just saw him at different times not too long ago," Cindy added.

"But that's him…my uncle. He is the one who died yesterday."

With those words from Oldpa the two ladies stood baffled and speechless. For about two minutes they all stood silently staring at each other's faces. Oldpa thought he had to say something to break the silence, but he could not come up with what to say. Then in an outburst the lady shouted, "Oh God, the man, so that is him, that was him. Wow!"

"Yes that was my uncle," Oldpa asserted.

"I can understand if you do not want to meet today," Cindy said. "I know how difficult this may be for you right now. Maybe we should leave you for now to grieve with your family."

"No, it's okay. We all knew he was going to die soon so we are not surprised. He had an internal bleeding problem he developed from the war. Many people especially those of us who were child soldiers live with some physical scars and pain. We can meet today if you want to interview me. It's no big deal. My people will understand."

"No, Oldpa, I really think we should postpone our meeting for today. I think you need the time to grieve with your family."

"It's okay," Oldpa insisted. "Our grieving period takes very long. It may go for a month or maybe more. We can meet in the little room over there." He pointed to a tiny door of a room that looked like it was only built to accommodate one person.

"Come in and have a seat, I will be right back," he told Cindy and her friend as he led the way.

As they entered the room he showed them two little chairs and told them to have a seat. He ran out of the room quickly yelling, "I will be back soon."

When Oldpa returned to the room he came with a jug of water and two sparkling glasses.

"We keep these glasses only for visitors," he said, smiling. "My uncle bought them and he never allowed any other person from our house to drink from them. He said they were for important visitors and one day he was going to prove to us that he knew very important people. But we all laughed at him every time he said that. My uncle was a good man and he lived well. I don't know why bad things always happen to good people."

The boy sat down on the chair that he had placed in front of Cindy when he said those words. He closed his eyes for about three seconds and then said to her, "Can I talk now? Are you ready?"

"Yes, yes, I am, whenever you are ready to talk. I am listening. Please do not feel like you only have to tell me your story as well. You can also say whatever is on your mind. Talk about your uncle and what he meant to you if you want. Just say anything that comes to your mind. I am listening."

"My uncle told me he wrote his story for you and your friend. He said that he told you in that story what happened at St. Peter's Church. Because you already know that story, I will tell you about what happened when I was a child soldier.

"I became a soldier at nine years old. I fought in so many wars in Liberia and in Sierra Leone. I was a strong fighter and so I was always on the war front. I was also a commander for the notorious Small Boys Unit or SBU.

"I didn't do many bad things to people when I was a soldier. I was always good to people because I wanted God to bless me. All the time I fought, there is only one thing that I did that still troubles my mind today. Even though my pastor says God has forgiven me, but I am still worried and my heart beats faster when I think about what I did."

"Would you mind to share it?" Cindy interrupted the boy.

"Yes, I don't mind to share it. In a town closer to Butuo where the war began, my unit was on patrol. We were scouting around when we came across an old man. The old man told us he had escaped the fighting and traveled to Ivory Coast with his family but he had to return to Liberia because his family had run out of food.

"He was a cocoa farmer who had returned to take the rest of his produce across the border to be sold. This is how he sustained his family until emergency food for refugees arrived.

"But when we met the old man his plan did not go well. I ordered one of my boys to kill him and they shot him. He died right there on the spot and we dragged his body into the high bush and just covered it with leaves.

"I dream about that old man no matter how many times I have prayed to God to forgive me. I see him in my dreams standing there at the same spot where the boys shot him and he is saying to me, 'My son, why did you kill me?'"

"But did the old man do anything wrong? What happened before you ordered your boys to kill him?" Cindy asked.

"When we met the old man I told him that we were in the town to protect them from intruders. I also told him we were taking care of the borders. I asked him to give us some money because my boys needed food. He told me he had no money. He sat down on the ground and said if we wanted to kill him we were welcome to do so, but he had no money to give to me. He later stood up and emptied the contents of his pocket. I asked him about the ring that he was wearing. He attempted to take off his ring but insisted that the ring could not come off because it was stuck to his finger. I pulled out my knife from my boot and threatened to cut the finger with the ring. But the old man, not wanting his finger to be cut off, quickly pulled the ring from his finger and gave it to me. I told him to take off his trousers. He took them off and that was when we found the money he had been hiding in the underpants he wore. I told him to leave the town and return to Ivory Coast. I told him I never wanted to see him again. I told him he was free to go. So we took all the money from him because he lied. But he did not leave the town. The next day he went to the quarter where the town commander lived."

"Wait, the town commander?" Cindy interrupted the boy again. "Who is that and how was his command different from you?"

"Every town had a commander but my unit moved from town to town. The town commanders did not have any power or rank to make us do anything, you see," he gestured with his hands, "because our ranks were higher. Our order came straight from the top, from the boss himself and no one else.

"The old man told the town commander that he had met some young kids who robbed him of his money and his ring. He tried to describe me to the town commander as a twelve-year-old kid who was very ruthless. He didn't know that my rank was higher than the town commander.

"When I walked out of the building where we slept, he shouted, 'There he is, the little boy that almost killed me.' His eyes were rolling and staring at everything in the army quarter, he seemed very disappointed when the town commander told him I was his boss. I knew he would have killed me if he had a gun. I was angry because he did not leave the town as I told him. I took my gun and ordered a few of my boys to come with me. I told the old man that we were going to escort him out of the quarter and out of the town. We escorted him out of the quarter but when we got in the forest, I was afraid he would have told another person that we robbed him. You never know who he might know.

"I wanted the old man to go in peace, you know. I wanted him to leave the town but then fear took hold of me. Because I saw him explaining to the town commander, I was not sure if he would have left the town and told another person the story. You never know the people some of these people know. He could have known someone that knows my boss. The whole thing could have come back to hurt me. I was scared...I was scared like hell and that's why I ordered my soldier to shoot him. I should have just let him go."

Oldpa said those last few words in tears. He buried his face in both hands and bowed his head, sobbing like a baby.

Cindy reached her hand over and patted his back. Then she said, "It was not your fault, Oldpa. It was not your fault. You were a child, a very young child who was misled by some older men. They destroyed your childhood just like they destroyed your uncle's childhood. Don't be too hard on yourself. It was not your fault."

Oldpa stopped crying and wiped his tears. He stared at Cindy's face blinking his eyes many more times than usual. Cindy's friend had been sitting all this while without saying a word. She reassured Oldpa saying, "It was not your fault as Cindy said. You need to move on and put that behind you. You were a child and people took advantage of you."

With those words from the lady, he slowly sat up straight and said, "But I did not kill the second old man."

"Was there another man there?" Cindy quickly asked.

"No, but we met another old man after that. He too was a cocoa farmer and he had come back to the country apparently for the same reason. For that man I just threatened him. When he attempted to make a complaint to the town commander, I told him he was wasting his time. I also told him there was nothing that could be done even if he met the chief of the town. I told him to leave the town and leave the country as quickly as possible.

"He took my words seriously and by the next day we heard he had left the country. He must have really run for his life. As a matter of fact we heard that he did not make it back to his house in the town and had sent words to his brother who was waiting for him at home that he was running for the river at the border crossing between Liberia and the Ivory Coast. He was going to board the canoe as quickly as possible and leave the country.

"'Tell him I can't wait or come back to the house,' his message said. 'Tell him my life has been threatened and I was told that if I was to be seen around here again, I would be killed. Tell him I am leaving and won't be back anytime soon to this country of ours.' Those were exactly the words that we heard that he had sent to his brother."

"Thank you, Oldpa, you have said a lot today and I also want to let you know that I have appreciated every single moment of our meeting and counseling time. I appreciate the telling of your story and the story from your uncle as well. We are very appreciative of our time that we spent in this country.

"We have decided that we will be leaving on Thursday, the day after tomorrow. Maybe we can meet tomorrow and go for dinner or do something together other than what we have usually done. Today though, I think you need to get some rest. You have done your best. You have been wonderful."

"Thank you, Oldpa, thank you," both the ladies said as they hugged the young boy who had been a former child soldier.

CHAPTER SIX

Night came to the city early on the day that Cindy had completed her final interview and counseling session with Oldpa. She knew that this day was coming and that the end of their journey to the West African country had come. The journey that began with her curiosity to learn about the psychological effect of war on children had taken a personal toll on her. She grabbed her back pack and squeezed it hard as she stood in the middle of her hotel room. She made a fist as though preparing for a fight, then retreated into a calm mood. She slowly and tenderly began labeling all the gifts she had receive from friends. On each gift she attached a piece of paper with the name of the item and the person that presented it to her. She placed each item in her suitcase one at a time until all of it was packed away.

She thought about what to do next after all the gifts were put away. Nothing immediately came to her mind. She has done quite a lot, she thought. Tomorrow was another day. The day when she would have to go to the agency she has worked with and thank the folks there and say goodbye to them, then meet with Oldpa for a dinner and run other errands. After a month and a half since arriving in the country, it was only a matter of hours now when she should be departing.

"The days go by so quickly, don't they?" she said to her friend who was still packing her suitcase.

"Certainly, they do," the lady replied.

"I am not sure if our trip here made any sense at all."

"What do you mean? I think it made sense. We had the opportunity to meet all these beautiful people and talk to child soldiers and war-affected children. Do you know how many people in the world would love to have an experience like ours, how many?"

"Yeah...I know but that's not what I am talking about. I mean, look at all these children and young boys and girls. What happen to them now? Look at Oldpa. When we leave here, it may be the last time we ever see him. Who knows what will happen to him next?

"I feel like we cheated them you know. Maybe the man was right or he is right when he said that all we do is come here and take their stories and make names for ourselves and forget about them. I feel like we are doing just that right now."

"Doing what, Cindy? Doing what?"

"Cheating them, you know. We are taking their stories with us. Even if we do not write a book we still write papers, don't we? We write theses and make presentations and talk of their stories as though it was ours."

"What are you talking about? Our coming here helped these people. If we don't tell their stories how do you expect the world to know? How do you propose their stories be told to those in Canada, for example, who sit at their breakfast and dinner table and all they hear about here is what they watch on television.

"We left our homes and our beds and came here. Doesn't that count? When we go back and make presentations on Oldpa and the other kids' stories, it could lead to someone sponsoring a child in this country or elsewhere with similar problem. Doesn't that count for something?

"I think you allowed the man to get to you with his writing. He was a smart man alright but he is all about politics too, you know? The first day I met him he spoke all politics. He tried to tell me about how colonization was continuing in another form.

"He said he thought that we were colonizers who have started to arrived to begin the process of modern-day colonization. He went on to say that we are like the missionaries that came to Africa with smiles on their faces, the Bibles in their right hands and the guns hidden behind them in their left hands. He tried to go as far as drawing an analogy between the war, their plight, our coming here and equate it to modern day slavery. That was the reason I had to stop him. I just couldn't take it anymore. I didn't quite get what he was trying to say but I thought to leave the topic because I knew where he was heading."

"You let him get to your head, Cindy, you did. You need to let all that stuff stay right here. You need to pack your bag and get some rest and prepare for tomorrow. Let's do all the errands we have to do and have a good night's sleep because we have a long flight ahead of us.

"You need to remind yourself that you have done your part. That you came to a country in West Africa in the hope that you could raise some awareness on their situations and that hopefully our so-called big government and wealthy people can help the children and the situation here. Look at us, we are only simple students who are struggling to pay our rent, less I say tuition. We barely have enough to keep ourselves in perfect health, what do you suppose we do?

"We are not professors or those big agencies and NGOs out there raising millions of dollars in the name of these people but doing nothing much to help them. Most of the agencies and NGOs are pretending to be the Good Samaritan but paying themselves fat salaries. They are not sincere and genuine. They do little to benefit the poor children in whom name they raise all that money."

"But that is exactly my point," Cindy asserted to her friend. "How sincere and genuine are we?"

"We came here very empty and yet we are going back with so much knowledge. Knowledge that we paid no money for except the plane ticket we bought to come here. They have impacted our lives and changed us forever. They have given us something that we will always be remembered for in our academic and personal lives. Yet to them we have given nothing, nothing at all."

CHAPTER SEVEN

Two weeks after Cindy and the lady returned to Canada she received an email to attend a conference on children in armed conflict situation. She immediately responded to the email saying that she very much appreciated the invitation but would first like to meet with the conference organizers prior to her acceptance. Her trip to West Africa to a conflict country where she had spoken to many child soldiers and war-affected children was overwhelming and she had some suggestions for the conference, the email concluded.

In the meeting with the conference organizers, Cindy suggested to them that she had spoken with a young man in West Africa whose story she found to be very interesting. She said she was sure that his story would be of interest to other participants and facilitators and then asked if the organizers could include a slot for the former child soldier.

"Include a slot, you mean bringing him physically to speak at this conference with only three months left to go?" one of the organizers asked.

"I mean exactly that," Cindy responded.

"But I do not see how we can do that, young lady. We do not just include slots into a program for a former child soldier who is halfway across the world. It took many months of preparations and thoughts to draw up the conference agenda. We cannot make sudden changes just like that."

"But you can suddenly decide to suddenly have a conference on child soldiers and war-affected children without actually inviting any of them? You think that's fair?"

"I don't know what you think you are doing, young lady, or should I say Cindy? We invited quite a number of children who will be attending this conference. You need to find out more information about the conference and

38

then let us help you with any other question you have."

When she said those few words, the lady got up to leave the meeting room, excusing herself from the meeting. As she attempted to walk through the door and into the long hallway leading to the stairs of the university auditorium, Cindy shouted for her to wait. She sat still for about two seconds and asked the lady, "How many of them are child soldiers?"

"Excuse me, I did not get that," the woman responded in a frantic voice.

"How many of the five children that were invited are actually child soldiers?"

"The children we invited are from within Canada. Now, I am not sure if any of them were child soldiers or not but we know that they and their parents originated from countries with major conflict where children are greatly affected."

"Conflict areas or countries with major conflict where children are greatly affected, that's it? I would assume that organizers of a conference with a theme 'how war affects children' and with a specific reference to 'child soldiers' as a sub-theme should be glad that someone offered to bring into the conference a former child soldier.

"A child soldier whose memory is still very fresh and lives with the pain almost every day. Look, I don't want us to go around this issue the whole time. I think that we can compromise and find a way where a five-minutes slot is included within the conference program for the young man I am hoping to invite."

"I think I am done here," the woman asserted as she took a glance at Cindy and then continued to walk away.

"No, you are not done," Cindy shouted. "We still have a whole lot to talk about. A whole lot indeed needs to be discussed. If you are done with me than I need someone that I can talk to about this situation."

She turned to the other organizer who remained sitting in her seat.

"I need to talk to someone else. Is there anyone else that I can talk to about this situation? Are you that person?"

"No, I am not that person," the other organizer responded. "But I need you to go home and get some rest and I promise I will get someone for you to talk to. I will give you a call when I do."

"Thank you," Cindy responded and quickly walked out of the room.

When Cindy got home, her friend, the lady, had come to see her. She waved at Cindy and said hello but she did not respond.

"Hey, what's up with you? You didn't even see me. I tried to get your attention but you just walked right pass me. Are you okay?"

"Not really! I went over to meet with the conference organizers about bringing over Oldpa to make a five-minute presentation and they wouldn't allow me to do so. Can you imagine that, five minutes and yet they tell me this is a conference about child soldiers."

"Actually I can imagine that," the lady told Cindy. "I can imagine how difficult it must be for them, you know? Planning this huge conference and trying to fit in a speaker who was not previously included in the program. Also, how sure can they be that Oldpa will say the right thing at the conference? You have to understand, Cindy, it's difficult for them. You can't just blame them or think that they are mean. I think they are only doing their jobs and being careful, that's all."

"That's exactly what all of you worry about, isn't it? Whether he will say the right thing or not? Or whether he will return to his country and not stay in Canada? Is there anything else you are worried about? How about if what he is going to say will fit into the academic context of the conference or if the academics will understand him? I heard all of these lines too, my friend. I have heard all of it and you know what, it doesn't bother me one bit. The reason is because all of you are concerned about the wrong issues as always.

"There are so many people in life facing real problems and instead of looking at what they faced on a daily basis, instead of finding real solutions to their problems, we make every effort to fit their issues into academic or policy contexts. I am not saying that it is necessarily a bad thing but I think we need to listen to people and hear their problems before we try to fix them. We can't continue to categorize their problems according to how we see fit.

"No wonder we in the developed world keep trying to fix the problems of the developing world and yet it keeps getting worse. We need to make people a part of the solution-finding process for their problems. And we can only do this if we are patient enough to listen to them. Only if we are not in a hurry to box their problems and give names and polish it to fit those names like academic and the rest."

"Wow, Cindy, where did you come from with all that stuff and how is it connected to bringing Oldpa to speak at this conference anyway?" the lady asserted. "You have surely been doing some intense reading or thinking I would imagine. I hear everything you just said and maybe you are right. I mean, who am I to say you are wrong, but one thing I can tell you for sure is that I strongly believe that in order to help people in the developing world, we have to design suitable methodology on how to fix their problems. We just can't listen to them. The way we design those suitable methodology is when we package their problems into categories. You must understand that there are others with similar problems and by categorizing we can find one solution for many problems. We can also learn best practices—"

"You mean like drawing up a single template that for some magical reason is supposed to be used to solve many different countries' problems. It's like the guide or manual I saw two weeks ago that was titled the *Guide to Project Management for Developing Countries?* This is a manual that is apparently supposed to be used by all Canadian development agencies to manage government projects overseas. The question that comes to my mind when I see books and manuals like these is what happens if a particular project does not fit into the ten or four guides or methods prescribed by these manuals and books? Are the managers supposed to fit the projects within the context of what that manual prescribes? I guess the simple answer is yes!

"You see we spent 300 days out of the 365 days a year designing methodologies, steps and models on how we should be fixing problems in the developing world and spent only sixty-five days actually solving the problems. No wonder we are always trying to fit problems and issues into pre-designed models instead of talking and listening to people and designing models to fit their problems."

"Whatever you say, Cindy, I guess you are right again."

The lady tried to avoid an argument with Cindy and had chosen just to listen to her speak her mind. When Cindy turned to the lady to begin another sentence, the phone rang. She ran for the phone and picked it up on the third ring.

"Hello, my name is Ted and I am the chair of the organizing committee for the conference coming up on how war affects children," the voice on the other end of the phone said. "Is this Cindy?"

"Yes, yes it is Cindy!"

"Well, I just called to let you know that your request to include a slot in the program for your young friend from West Africa to speak has been granted. But please be sure to get him here at the latest one week before the conference. Can you do that?"

"Yes, yes, Mr. Ted, or should I say Ted, yes, I can do that. And…and I just really want to say thank you very much. Thank you and like my grandmother always say to people, may the Lord bless you abundantly."

"Oh, thank you, Cindy, that's very kind of you. But anyway, you can just call me Ted. Ted is fine. I look forward to seeing you and your friend when he gets here. But please do not hesitate to give us a call if there is anything we can do to help. We will also be checking with you again in a month from now to find out what has happened if you have not called us by then. Have a great day and good luck!"

When Cindy dropped the phone she shouted with extreme joy and ran towards her friend.

"Yes! Yes! Yes! I can bring Oldpa over for the conference. Oh my God, I am so happy. I am so thankful to God. Maybe I should call Oldpa now and let him know. What time will it be there in his country? I hope he will be willing to come. I really hope that he will be willing to take this opportunity to share his story himself with the world. I hope he will be as excited as I am right now."

CHAPTER EIGHT

When Cindy contacted Oldpa about sharing his story with a group in Canada he screamed in excitement and expressed a sign of happiness. But he was quick to calm himself down and looked around him to see if anyone had noticed his excitement. There were many people seated outside of the small booth where he had come to receive the call from Cindy. Like him thousands of other families in the war-torn country had no phone of their own. Small phone booths were set up by those who could afford phone service. Before Cindy and her friend left the country, she had asked for the number of the phone booth close to Oldpa's house. Her request was now proving useful. She called the number and asked to speak with Oldpa and someone had run over to his house to tell him he had a phone call.

Unlike many other people who sit by the booth for the whole day waiting to see if a relative or friend from the United States or Canada would call them, Oldpa had not received any calls from anyone prior to Cindy called. He always walked by and saw many people seated by the phone booth chatting. Sometimes he took a moment to stop and chat with some friends but he knew he did not have any relatives or friends in the United States or Canada to call him. So he never sat by the booth. But as he stood in the booth talking to Cindy, he knew that he would have many people watching him out of curiosity. He knew that as soon as he stepped out of the booth some of his friends would ask him immediately about who had called him and possibly about his excitement. Oldpa calmed himself and said to Cindy that she was different and that she was not like all of the other so-called researcher who came before her.

"I wish my uncle was alive," he said with his face lighting up. "I always told him that you seemed to be a very genuine woman and that we could trust you.

Your effort now proves just that. So when will I be coming?" he asked in a delighted voice.

"Soon, very soon, but we will have to process your visa application and other requirements first. Do you have a passport?"

"No, I don't have one. It costs a lot of money to get a passport."

"Don't worry about the money, Oldpa. I will send you some money to begin processing your passport," Cindy said to assure the boy. "How soon are you able to get your passport?"

"I don't know. I will have to ask about that."

"Great! Why don't you ask about how long it will take you to get a passport? Are you able to do that within two days? Can I call you back on Thursday to find out if you were able to get an answer?"

"Yes, Thursday! Call back on Thursday and I will be able to give you an answer."

"Okay, Oldpa, it was nice talking to you today. I will call you back on Thursday. Hope you have a wonderful day."

But just before the phone went dead Cindy shouted, "Remember, Oldpa, we have very short time to do this so please find out the information before I call back. Actually I have only two months to get you here."

Cindy remembered that just saying "I will do it" did not mean that it was going to be done. In Liberia like many other developing countries, it was easier to commit to something than actually take the time to do it.

She thought that taking the time to remind Oldpa would help him realized the urgency of time. She knew that though he might be aware that time was of the essence, the usual way of doing things where he lived would prevent him from acting with urgency. She hoped that those last few words would help him act quickly.

When Oldpa dropped the phone he wasted no time in contacting friends and asking how he could get a passport and how long it would take. Most of the friends he asked had no specific answer for him but one of them had mentioned to him that his father works at the Ministry of Foreign Affairs.

"Foreign Affairs, is that where we get passport?"

"I don't know," his friend answered, "but I know my father brought home some passports for some of his friends before. Let's go to my house and ask my mom," he suggested.

Oldpa asked his friend's mom if there was any possibility to get a passport from her husband even though he had no money.

"We will see what we can do," his friend's mom asserted. "But what do you need the passport for?"

Oldpa explained to his friend's mom that a Canadian friend of his was inviting him to Canada for a conference and that she had asked him to get a passport. She was going to call back in two days to find out if he knew where and how to get the passport. He also needed to know how long it was going to take to get a passport since his Canadian friend only had two months to process his paper.

He struggled to persuade his friend's mother as he switched from one story to the other about how he met Cindy and how their relationship got to where it was. He told her that Cindy was a mere friend he had met while she was conducting her research. But his friend's mother did not seem to be buying Oldpa's story. She had seen how most of the white women who came to conduct research or work with international NGOs fell in love with the local boys, married them and took them away. She was convinced Oldpa had met one of those white women and was now preparing to leave the country to join her in Canada.

"So what are you going to do about my little niece, Oldpa?"

"What, who is your little niece?" Oldpa asked in a frantic voice.

"My niece is the girl that you live with, your girlfriend, and I asked the question I asked because many of you marry these white women, leave with them and you forget the girls that you live with. You forget your very own local girls that live and endure hardship for you. So, please tell me what you are going to do about my niece. I am willing to ask my husband help you get the passport but you have to tell me your plans for my niece."

Oldpa stood baffled for a few seconds and then responded with a chuckle as though to reassure himself that he knew this was coming. But deep in his mind he was also trying hard to control his anger. These were the moments that brought back memories of his soldier years. Those years when no one, not even the oldest person on earth, would question him or his motives. For he was a soldier, or maybe an equivalent of the United States Marine and at the time he was told civilians had no right to question him. But those days were gone now. Times had changed and he was a different man.

"Oh, I am sorry. I didn't know she was your niece. She never told me," he said to his friend's mother.

"Well, now you know. But you still have to answer my other question. What is your intention for her or what are your plans? Are you going to leave now and go to Canada to your white woman and forget about her? Leave her here with the baby and that's it?"

"No, I am not married to any white woman. She is only a friend. She wants me to speak at a conference in Canada. I will only be gone for two weeks and I will be back."

The conversation did not last too long. When Oldpa seemed to reassure his friend's mother that he was not one of those local young men who married a white woman, she propped up her shoulder and promised with hesitation that she would consider helping him.

"Come back later this afternoon when my husband comes back from work," she said.

But Oldpa did not just walk away. He looked the woman straight into the eye and said, "I never got married to my Canadian friend. She came here for research. She was conducting research with former child soldiers. That's how we met. She interviewed me and now she wants me to share the same story I shared with her with other people, that's all."

When Cindy called after two days Oldpa told her the family that lived down the street from him could help him get the passport in one week but it would require about US $500.00. He also mentioned to her that he had no money and earning US $500.00 would take him the next year and a half, even if he was to work two jobs every day of the week. But Cindy quickly interrupted Oldpa and said she would send him the money to get the passport.

"I managed to raise some money to enable us make your visit here possible," she said. "I hosted dinners, held fundraisers at various bars and night clubs and asked friends for donations. So far I have been able to raise $8,000.00. This is good news, Oldpa, so I hope you will be willing to meet some of my friends who contributed and made your trip possible. Would you be willing to do that, to meet some of the people who helped to pay for your trip?"

"Yes, I will be willing to do that."

"Thanks, Oldpa! I will send you the money for the passport first thing tomorrow morning. I will also send some extra money to buy some new clothes for yourself and have some extra cash on you. I am sure we have enough money to cover your expenses even while you are here. Let's hope though that there will be some cash left for you to take back with you and establish a business or something. What do you thing?

"I was told one of the usual and fastest ways to send money is through the Western Union. Do you have any identification to be able to claim the money I send tomorrow?"

"Yes, I have an ID card."

"Okay, good! Check any Western Union close to you tomorrow and the money will be there."

"Thank you, Cindy! Thank you very much. But when will I be coming?"

"Don't know the exact time yet, Oldpa. But we have got to work on the most difficult aspect of getting you here. That is getting a visa for you."

"Do you think I will get a visa? I heard it is very difficult to get one." Oldpa's voice sounded shaky and scared when he spoke about the visa.

"Remember nothing is too difficult, Oldpa. We are in this together and I will do everything it takes to make this happen."

The words of encouragement from Cindy not only strengthened Oldpa's resolve, it reminded him of a very special moment in his life during the civil war. He was shot and wounded in a battle for a town where enemy forces overran his unit. Almost at the point of death, he woke up a week later in a house where he came to know the owner as Mama Sarah. A widow who husband was killed in the war, Mama Sarah had three children and had been displaced three times. She told Oldpa when he woke up that he was badly wounded but she had treated his wound. She told him not to worry because no situation was too difficult to be fixed. Though she explained to him that his wound was life-threatening, she also said to him that they were in it together and that she would do anything it took to save his life.

For Oldpa, Mama Sarah could never be forgotten. When she died he did everything he could to pay for her funeral. He told her children that she was his mother too and that he was going to take charge of her funeral expenses. He could afford to do so at the time because he was a soldier. And he did. Her funeral lasted for a week and it was memorable. The songs and worships ceremonies were all designed to keep a spiritual environment until one event.

When the singing and the worship at the funeral were over and the preacher had been asked to come to the pulpit, he took the stand and began to tell the people about the good deeds of Mama Sarah. Suddenly a young man stood up. He was seated in the back row of the seats allocated for sympathizers. But he slowly made his way to the front towards the pulpit and then asked to be allowed to speak. People shouted at him to sit down. Some said he was drunk and should not be allowed closer to the pulpit. But the young man made his way to the pulpit without allowing the noise and the shouting to distract him. The preacher watched him lift up his right hand as though asking for permission. Then the preacher decided to let him speak.

The young man stood at the pulpit staring and lingering as though he was going to fall down. He looked up at the crowd, stretched forth his right hand towards the preacher and said, "Thank you." Then with spit drooling out of his mouth, he said, "Mama Sarah was indeed a very generous woman. The woman was so generous that she even let me sample a portion of her delight. What a woman, yeah…what a woman. That is all I wanted to say."

Cindy's encouraging words got Oldpa thinking about Mama Sarah when he dropped the phone. But of course he also remembered the event that produced some laughter in the midst of all the sadness.

CHAPTER NINE

In Winnipeg, when the conference began, Cindy was there but Oldpa had not arrived in Canada. Because of the delay it took to convince embassy officials for his visa, he left his home country a day before the conference began. Cindy was confident he would make it safely. She knew he was somewhere in transit in Europe or at least that is what she thought. She held her breath and hoped for the morning to come early. She held her confidence and waited patiently as she sat through the first day of the conference. From one participant to the other the five-day conference was crowded with academics, practitioners and policy makers. However, Cindy's attempt to quietly sit through the first day of the conference did not succeed. During lunch time, the chair of the organizing committee waved at her and asked if she could follow him to the secretariat.

"So what do you think so far?" he asked rhetorically, adjusting the chair for her to sit down. "Do you like what you see? I thought the first speaker this morning was quite eloquent and knowledgeable. That is exactly what we intended for this conference and I am glad we began on that note.

"So can I get to meet with you and your friend later today? Is he around? I actually expected that you were going to contact me prior to today to meet with you and your friend."

"I tried to contact you two days ago," Cindy asserted. "But I was told you were very busy preparing for the conference and the staff I spoke with could not say when you would be free. But I wanted to let you know that due to delays in processing his visa, Oldpa will get here tomorrow. He arrives in the morning and I promise to bring him straight to the conference as soon as he gets here."

"That's fine! I hope one day is enough time for him to go over what we prepared for him."

"Prepared for him?" Cindy asked.

"Yes, Cindy, we had to prepare what we think he should say especially when he speaks at the main hall. Did you have something else in mind?"

"Well isn't that a question that you should have asked me earlier? I went through all this hassle to get him here and then I have no say in what he presents at the conference? How terrible do you people behave?"

"First I had to deal with this really mean woman on your staff who swore that I could not get Oldpa here to speak at the conference—thank God the other staff was nice enough and she contacted you, and then now his speech at the conference had been prepared without my knowledge? I don't get it? What are you people up to?"

"We are not up to anything. I just thought that you and Old…how do you say his name again?"

"Oldpa."

"…Oldpa will prepare and share at two workshops without our inputs, but whatever he speaks in the main hall we have to decide. I hope this arrangement is okay with you?"

"Sure, thanks! Do I have a choice at this late stage? If I say no, then what happens?"

"I hope you do not say no, Cindy. I hope you understand."

"Of course I understand! Anything else you want me to know?"

"Not at this time. If anything changes, I will make sure to let you know."

"Okay, I hope you enjoy the rest of today but please do not forget to bring your friend straight to the conference secretariat as soon as he gets here."

"Will do!"

Cindy got up and shook hands with the chair for the organizing committee. "I think I should get going because I have few things to complete before the afternoon session of the conference begins. Thank you again," she said, running her way out. Her voice was faint through the long hallway leading to the main hall.

The afternoon session of the conference began with invigorating speeches. One speaker said, "We need to ensure that countries reform their laws to seek the welfare of children to a greater extent." Another said, "Too many children are traumatized and as such, NGOs working with them in various areas need to be funded to meet the needs of these children. It is my hope that at the end of this conference we will have come up with concrete ways in which our governments or policymakers can begin to think alike with practitioners who are on the ground." Speech after speech and one phrase after the other. The few young people invited to the conference sat in their seats silently, listening and periodically talking to one another in low tones.

But this conference wanted to make a difference. The organizers realized there was the need to ask a young person, a war-affected child or former child soldier, to speak. The least that they could do was ask one child who had suffered the tragedies of war to speak for all the others, and Cindy brought them to do that. They would say to him or her, "Come on, take the stage, speak, tell us what the children are going through. Speak, don't be afraid."

Cindy's effort to remind all these older folks or conference participants always speaking on behalf of the children had a pay-off. Her desire to show disconnection between the policies and the actual situations was becoming fruitful. She managed to persuade the conference that academics and policy makers cannot always speak for the children. They can't always put their situations in the academic context and certainly they cannot always make huge policies based on theories. There is a greater need to listen to the raw facts that academics will omit from their presentations because of "ethical" reasons or policy makers detach because it is not in the government interest. Given the chance the children, the young boys and girls would say the nasty details themselves.

Now was that time, she thought to herself. She hoped Oldpa would be as bold as he was to her in West Africa when she first met him. She hoped that in the few minutes he had to speak, that he would give these folks the nasty details and attitude he had shown her in Liberia. She hoped he would exercise that boldness in front of all these people. The boldness that his uncle had told him to exercise on her. She hoped he would make her proud but most of all she hoped he would represent the millions and millions of voiceless children living in the shadow of older folks.

When it was time for him to speak, Oldpa took the stage and began reading with boldness what he was told to read. It was the prepared speech he had been made to read over and over since he got off the plane, neatly typed in bold letters so that he saw every word. He had had no time to change the clothes he was wearing. He was driven from the airport and given some food. Then he spent the rest of the morning and afternoon going over the five-minute speech.

The next morning, he took the stage, opened the file folder and without hesitation began reading the script he was given. But three paragraphs into the speech he paused, looked around him and said, "Wait…I must say something. I cannot read all these big words. I want to say what they did to my friends and me. I want to say something on behalf of my friends, my brothers and those that were killed right next to me and my sister too."

"No! Not now, Oldpa." One of the conference organizers was appointed to stand next to the podium as he read. She stood there to help him with words he could not pronounce correctly. They must have anticipated that something of this nature would happen.

"No, not now, Oldpa," she repeated. "Look, everybody is watching you. Read what's on the paper first. Once you are done, then we will find a way for you to speak about your friends. Maybe in one of your workshops, you can talk about your friends. Cindy will work with you and you will have lots of time to do just that," the organizer said in low tone closer to his ears.

But instead of taking the organizer's advice and continuing on with the prepared speech, he stood still and began sobbing. All the participants said, "Oh…look, it must be really difficult for him. It is so sad! He cannot even read the speech without sobbing. That little boy must be hurt." But in a short moment that produced the conference's greatest surprise the little boy lifted up his head and wiped the tears running down his cheeks. His face lit up with a bold look in his eyes. He closed the file folder with the prepared speech and stood still for a few seconds. And then like a lioness standing her ground for her cubs he said, "We, the children, young boys and girls or whatever name you want to call us, suffer terribly in war and after the war. We did not only become slaves to those who forced us to fight, we became slaves to ourselves.

"I would have loved to grow up normally as a child and slowly make my way into adulthood. I would have loved to walk on the beach with my girlfriend holding hands. Instead I was given a gun at the age of nine.

"Like me many other children suffered and continued to suffer. For us it is a lose-lose chance. There is really no second chance, no second life. We were killed even before we were born. When we suffered the deadliest attacks, both from our enemies during battles and then from our own fighting forces, when loyalty is forced upon us and they make us do all the worse things like killing each other and killing families we know, we lost our minds even before we can develop it. We cannot say no.

"They used us for deadly missions, often collecting intelligence that led to our capture or death. We cannot refuse! We never refuse because we would be killed, or our fingers cut off or our arms amputated. I lost my middle finger on my left hand because my commander said I left my assignment at one checkpoint. These days I have nine fingers.

"I have a friend who like many of the other children could not come to this conference because he was not invited, but he told me to tell you his story. It is a very short story. Please bear with me. He told me to tell you that when he was caught, they tied his hands. And then he and the other children were told to kill another girl with a stick, who tried to run away. He had never killed a woman before so he felt sick, he said. He refused to kill the girl, but they pointed guns at him, so he did it. But throughout the event the girl was asking him, 'Why are you doing this? Why are you killing me?' After they killed the girl, the older folks told them to smear her blood on their arms. They said to them, it was for bravery.

"My friend said to tell you he still dreams of the girl who was killed in cold blood. 'I see her in my dreams all the time and she is asking me why I killed her,' he said."

The boy had barely finished the story when half the conference participants were wiping tears from their eyes. But he never allowed the crying from some of the conference participants to stop him.

"I may be here today to speak to you, but there are thousands of other children, young boys and girls, who suffered more pain than I have. Their voices are never heard because every day people, especially older folks, shut them up. No one listens to them but every day we hear about the efforts being made on behalf of children. Please give us the chance to tell you our story.

"Like me, many children, young boys and girls out there are growing up naked. And this is a really bad thing for the future of our world. We are going to have a world full with naked people in the future if nothing serious is done to stop this. You can imagine what it means.

"I do not mean naked as you may want to imagine. I mean naked in our hearts and minds and souls. Your efforts may help heal our physical bodies, put clothes on us and feed us but inside we are still cold and hungry and dying."

In the distance, Cindy stood wiping her own tears from her face. She tried to look up at Oldpa and catch a glimpse of his face as he was leaving the podium. She knew he had stood his ground with boldness and said some of the things he wanted to say to the world. But she also knew that there were many other things lingering inside his mind that his dead uncle would have loved for him to say. But that did not matter much now. Maybe the rest could be said in a book that two of them might write together someday. For now she was about to embark on a long journey back to West Africa where uncertainty awaited her.

Maybe it was time that she faced the reality that she had always told others about in this trouble country, or worse, be caught in harm's way. The temptation to allow fear to overtake her and stay at home was high. But for now it seemed like she had lost the battle to stay home within herself.

In the coming week she was going to pack her suitcases and bags and after she had introduced Oldpa to some families and friends. They would be leaving for the airport, heading home. As she hugged Oldpa and thanked him for his bravery and boldness on the podium, she slowly and softly uttered the title of the book she thought they might write together.

When Oldpa looked her in her eye, she said, "Maybe we can write a book together and title it, *Growing Up Naked: The Untold Stories of Children at War.*"